W9-CLJ-533

# HAN SOLO: VOLUME 5

*It is a period of unrest. In a galaxy oppressed by the Empire's merciless cruelty, there is little hope for the future. Nonetheless, rebels have banded together to fight back against corruption.*

*Untrusting by nature, Han Solo has taken a step back from the rebel cause, returning his focus to what he does best—smuggling. However, when Princess Leia approaches him with an offer too good to refuse, Han finds himself racing the Millennium Falcon in one of the most notorious races in the galaxy, the Dragon Void, as a cover to find a suspected rebel traitor.*

After a series of close run-ins with the Empire, all three Alliance informants—and potential suspects—are now aboard the *Falcon*. Now, Han must discover the identity of the spy while completing the race—but the traitor has already started killing....

**MARJORIE LIU**
Writer

**MARK BROOKS**
Artist

**SONIA OBACK**
Colors

**KAMOME SHIRAHAMA**
Cover Artist

**VC's JOE CARAMAGNA**
Letterer

**HEATHER ANTOS**
Assistant Editor

**JORDAN D. WHITE**
Editor

**C.B. CEBULSKI**
Executive Editor

**AXEL ALONSO**
Editor In Chief

**JOE QUESADA**
Chief Creative Officer

**DAN BUCKLEY**
Publisher

For Lucasfilm:
Creative Director **MICHAEL SIGLAIN**
Senior Editor **FRANK PARISI**
Lucasfilm Story Group **RAYNE ROBERTS, PABLO HIDALGO, LELAND CHEE, MATT MARTIN**

ABDO
Spotlight

## ABDOPUBLISHING.COM

Reinforced library bound edition published in 2018 by Spotlight,
a division of ABDO, PO Box 398166, Minneapolis, Minnesota 55439.
Spotlight produces high-quality reinforced library bound editions for
schools and libraries. Published by agreement with Marvel Characters, Inc.

Printed in the United States of America, North Mankato, Minnesota.
042017
092017

THIS BOOK CONTAINS
RECYCLED MATERIALS

marvelkids.com

## STAR WARS © & TM 2017 LUCASFILM LTD.

## PUBLISHER'S CATALOGING IN PUBLICATION DATA

Names: Liu, Marjorie, author. | Brooks, Mark ; Oback, Sonia ; Milla, Matt,
   illustrators.
Title: Han Solo / writer: Marjorie Liu ; art: Mark Brooks ; Sonia Oback ; Matt Milla.
Description: Reinforced library bound edition. | Minneapolis, Minnesota : Spotlight,
   2018. | Series: Star wars : Han Solo | Volumes 1, 2, 3, and 5 written by Marjorie
   Liu ; illustrated by Mark Brooks, & Sonia Oback. | Volume 4 written by Marjorie
   Liu ; illustrated by Mark Brooks, Sonia Oback, & Matt Milla.
Summary: When Princess Leia approaches him with an offer too good to refuse,
   Han Solo finds himself flying in one of the galaxy's most dangerous races, the
   Dragon Void, as a cover to find a mysterious rebel spy who may have turned
   traitor.
Identifiers: LCCN 2017931205 | ISBN 9781532140150 (volume 1) | ISBN
   9781532140167 (volume 2) | ISBN 9781532140174 (volume 3) | ISBN
   9781532140181 (volume 4) | ISBN 9781532140198 (volume 5)
Subjects: LCSH: Solo, Han (Fictitious character)--Juvenile fiction. | Space warfare--
   Juvenile fiction. | Adventure and adventurers--Juvenile fiction. | Comic book,
   strips, etc.--Juvenile fiction. | Graphic novels--Juvenile fiction.
Classification: DDC 741.5--dc23
LC record available at https://lccn.loc.gov/2017931205

**Spotlight**

A Division of ABDO
abdopublishing.com

STAR WARS

# HAN SOLO

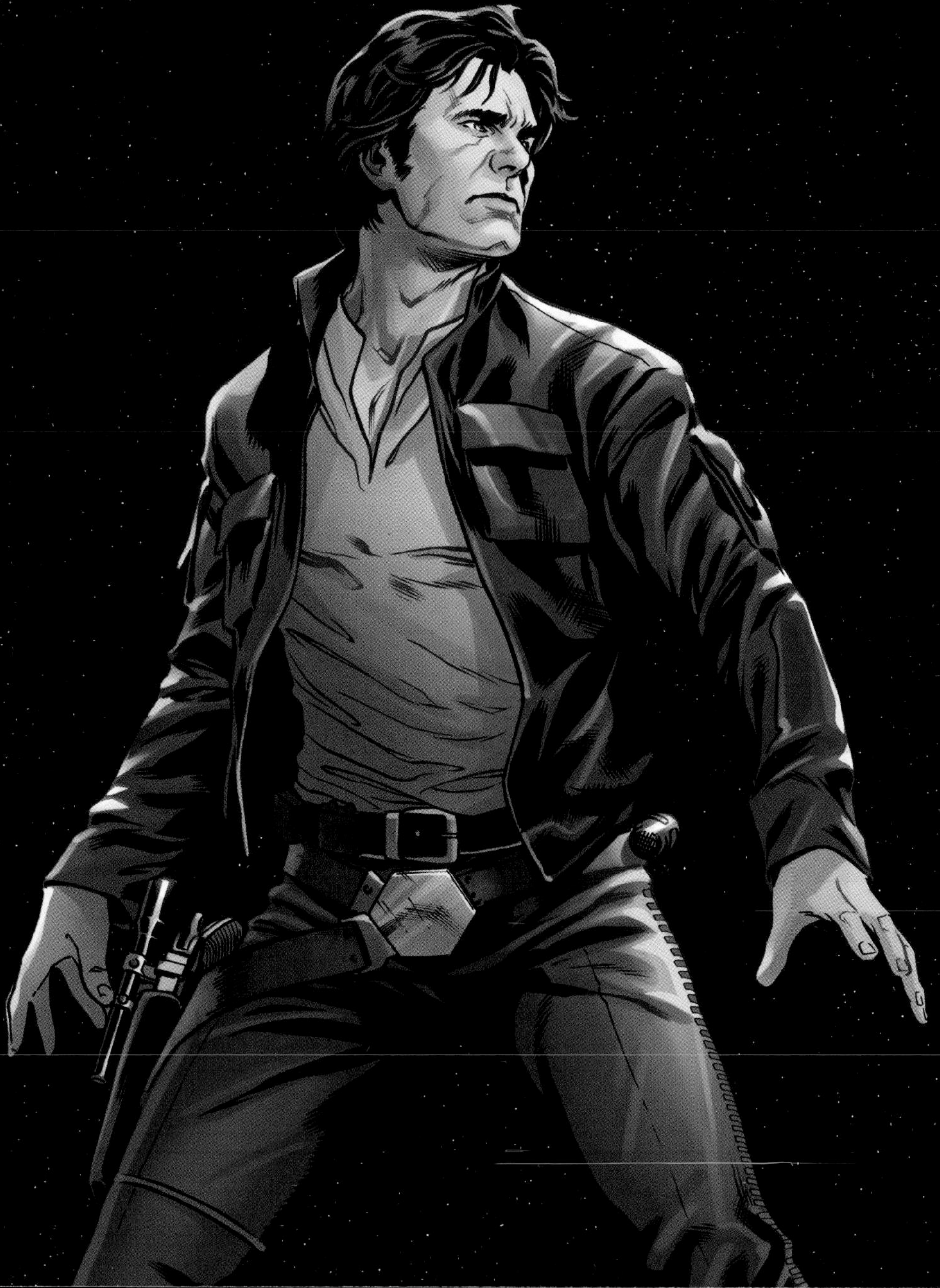

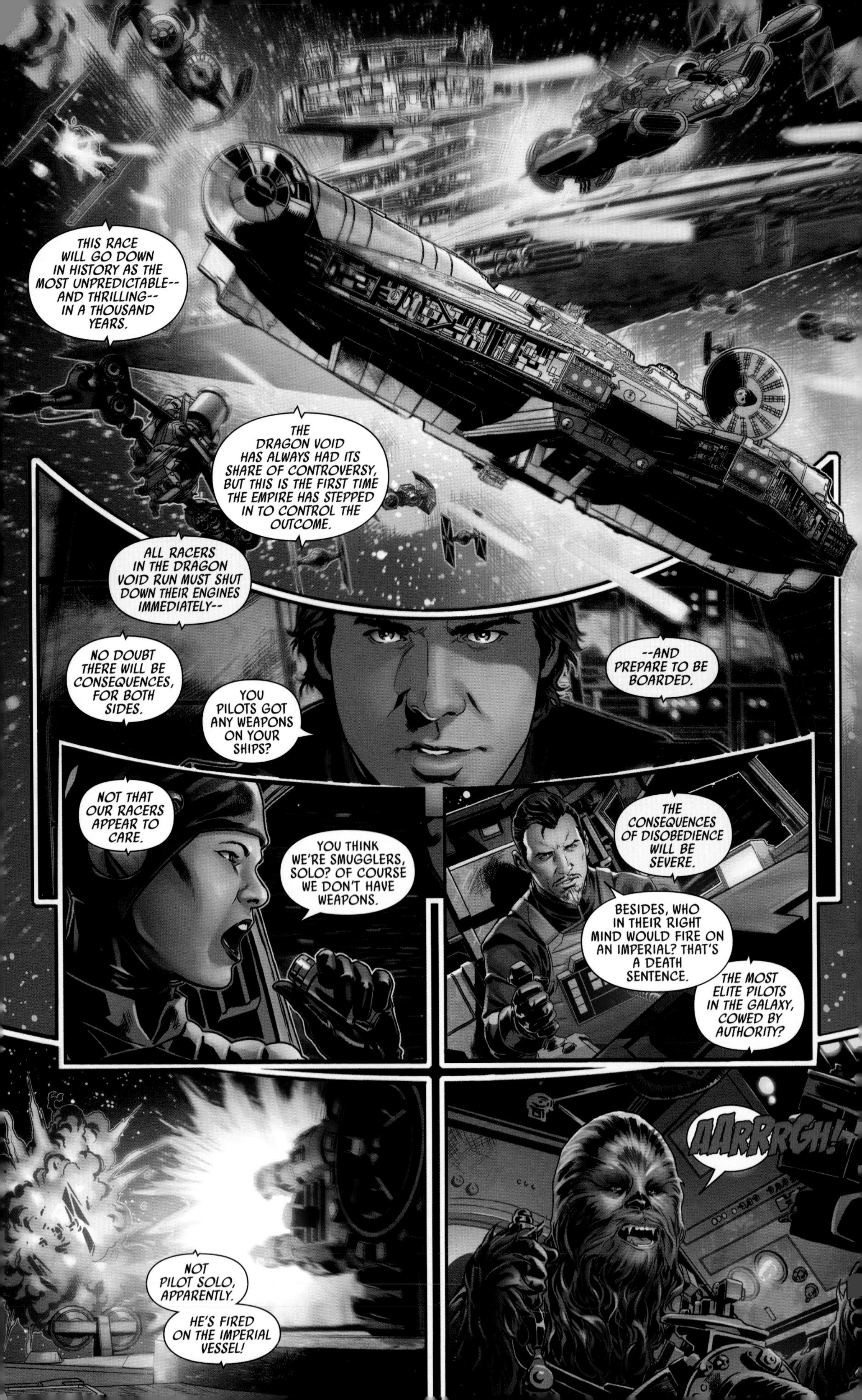
THIS RACE WILL GO DOWN IN HISTORY AS THE MOST UNPREDICTABLE-- AND THRILLING-- IN A THOUSAND YEARS.
THE DRAGON VOID HAS ALWAYS HAD ITS SHARE OF CONTROVERSY, BUT THIS IS THE FIRST TIME THE EMPIRE HAS STEPPED IN TO CONTROL THE OUTCOME.
ALL RACERS IN THE DRAGON VOID RUN MUST SHUT DOWN THEIR ENGINES IMMEDIATELY--
NO DOUBT THERE WILL BE CONSEQUENCES, FOR BOTH SIDES.
YOU PILOTS GOT ANY WEAPONS ON YOUR SHIPS?
--AND PREPARE TO BE BOARDED.
NOT THAT OUR RACERS APPEAR TO CARE.
YOU THINK WE'RE SMUGGLERS, SOLO? OF COURSE WE DON'T HAVE WEAPONS.
THE CONSEQUENCES OF DISOBEDIENCE WILL BE SEVERE.
BESIDES, WHO IN THEIR RIGHT MIND WOULD FIRE ON AN IMPERIAL? THAT'S A DEATH SENTENCE.
THE MOST ELITE PILOTS IN THE GALAXY, COWED BY AUTHORITY?
NOT PILOT SOLO, APPARENTLY.
HE'S FIRED ON THE IMPERIAL VESSEL!
AARRRGH!

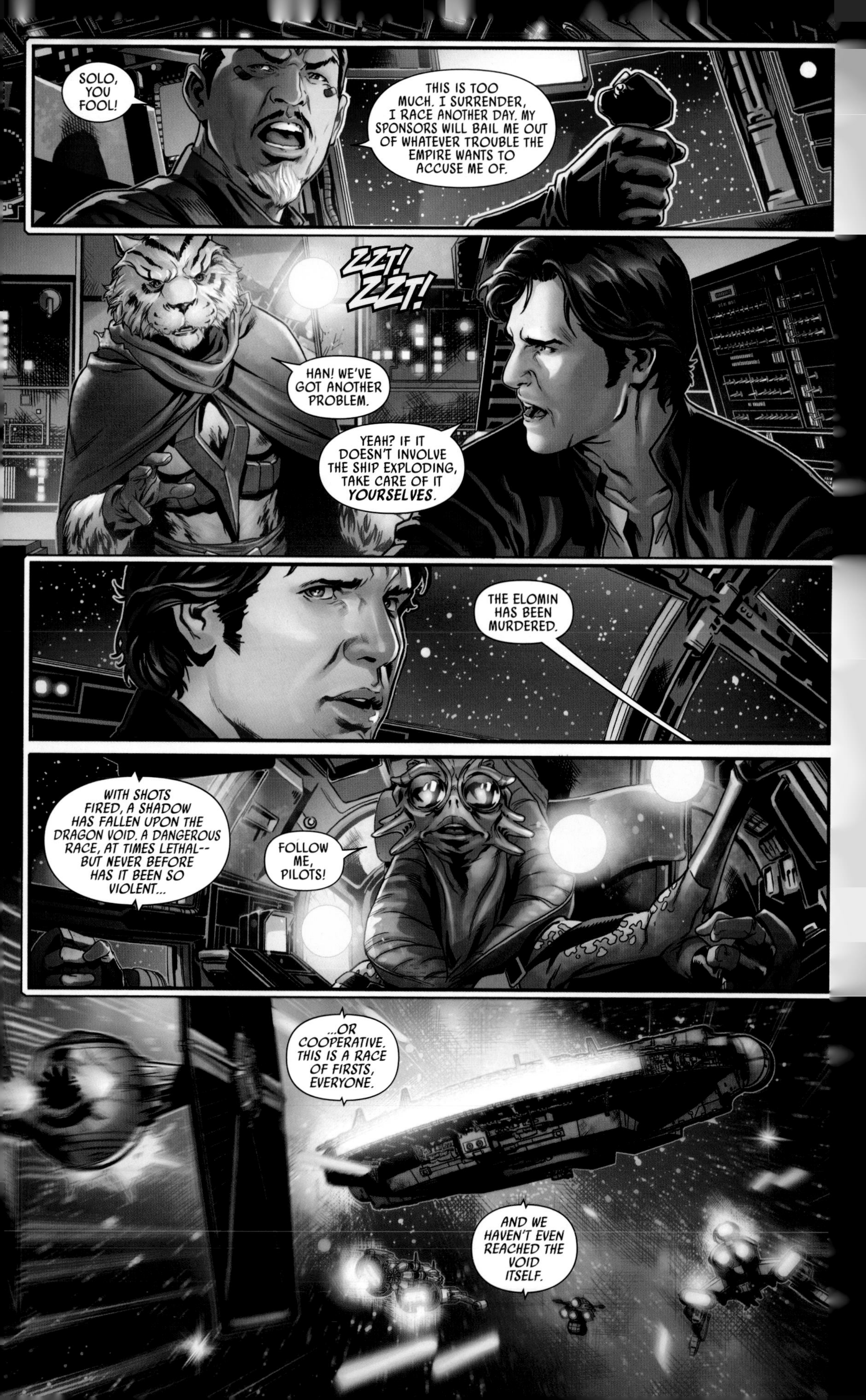
SOLO, YOU FOOL!
THIS IS TOO MUCH. I SURRENDER, I RACE ANOTHER DAY. MY SPONSORS WILL BAIL ME OUT OF WHATEVER TROUBLE THE EMPIRE WANTS TO ACCUSE ME OF.
ZZT! ZZT!
HAN! WE'VE GOT ANOTHER PROBLEM.
YEAH? IF IT DOESN'T INVOLVE THE SHIP EXPLODING, TAKE CARE OF IT *YOURSELVES.*
THE ELOMIN HAS BEEN MURDERED.
WITH SHOTS FIRED, A SHADOW HAS FALLEN UPON THE DRAGON VOID. A DANGEROUS RACE, AT TIMES LETHAL-- BUT NEVER BEFORE HAS IT BEEN SO VIOLENT...
FOLLOW ME, PILOTS!
...OR COOPERATIVE. THIS IS A RACE OF FIRSTS, EVERYONE.
AND WE HAVEN'T EVEN REACHED THE VOID ITSELF.

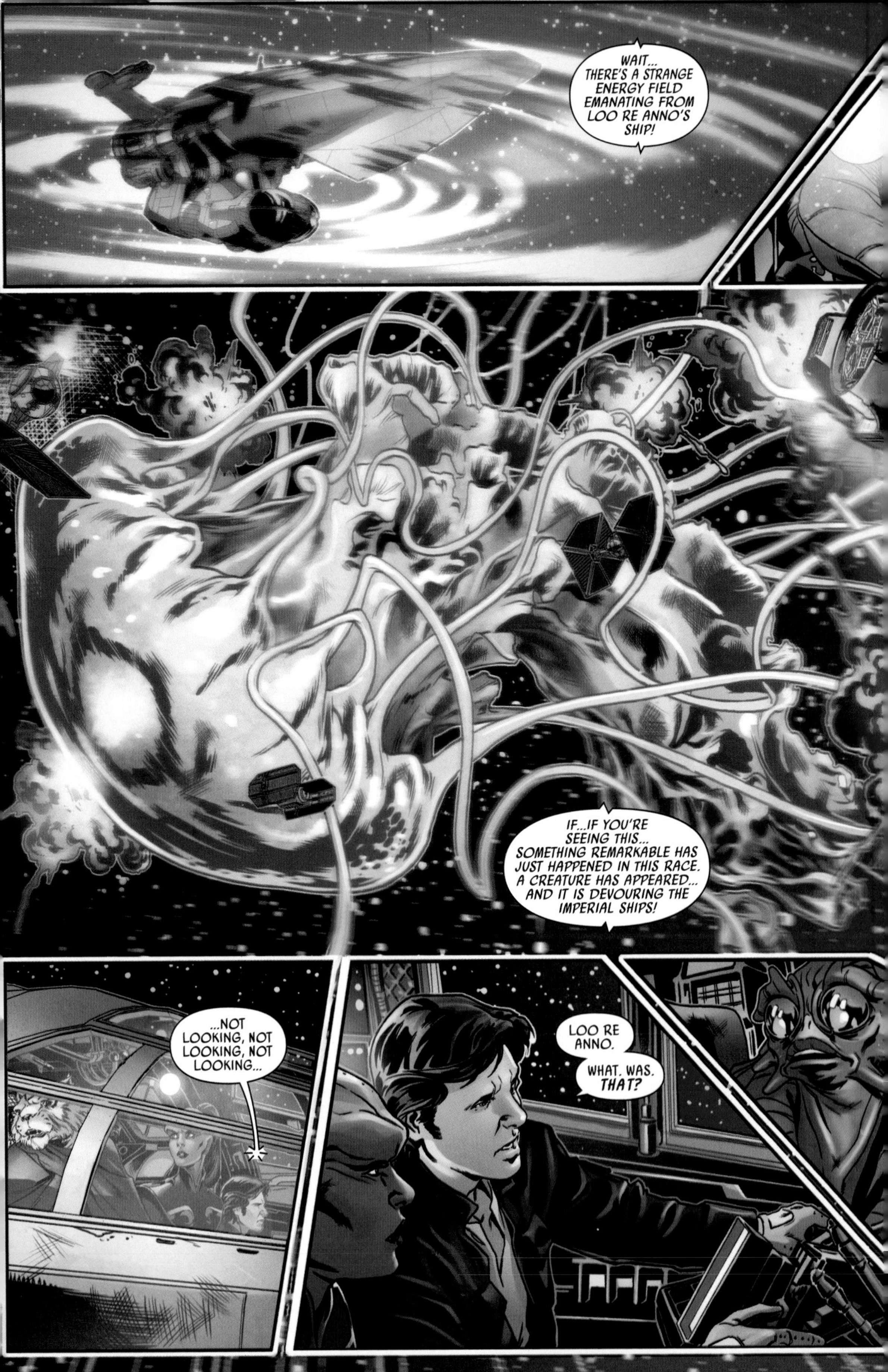

WAIT... THERE'S A STRANGE ENERGY FIELD EMANATING FROM LOO RE ANNO'S SHIP!
IF...IF YOU'RE SEEING THIS... SOMETHING REMARKABLE HAS JUST HAPPENED IN THIS RACE. A CREATURE HAS APPEARED... AND IT IS DEVOURING THE IMPERIAL SHIPS!
...NOT LOOKING, NOT LOOKING, NOT LOOKING...
LOO RE ANNO.
WHAT. WAS. THAT?

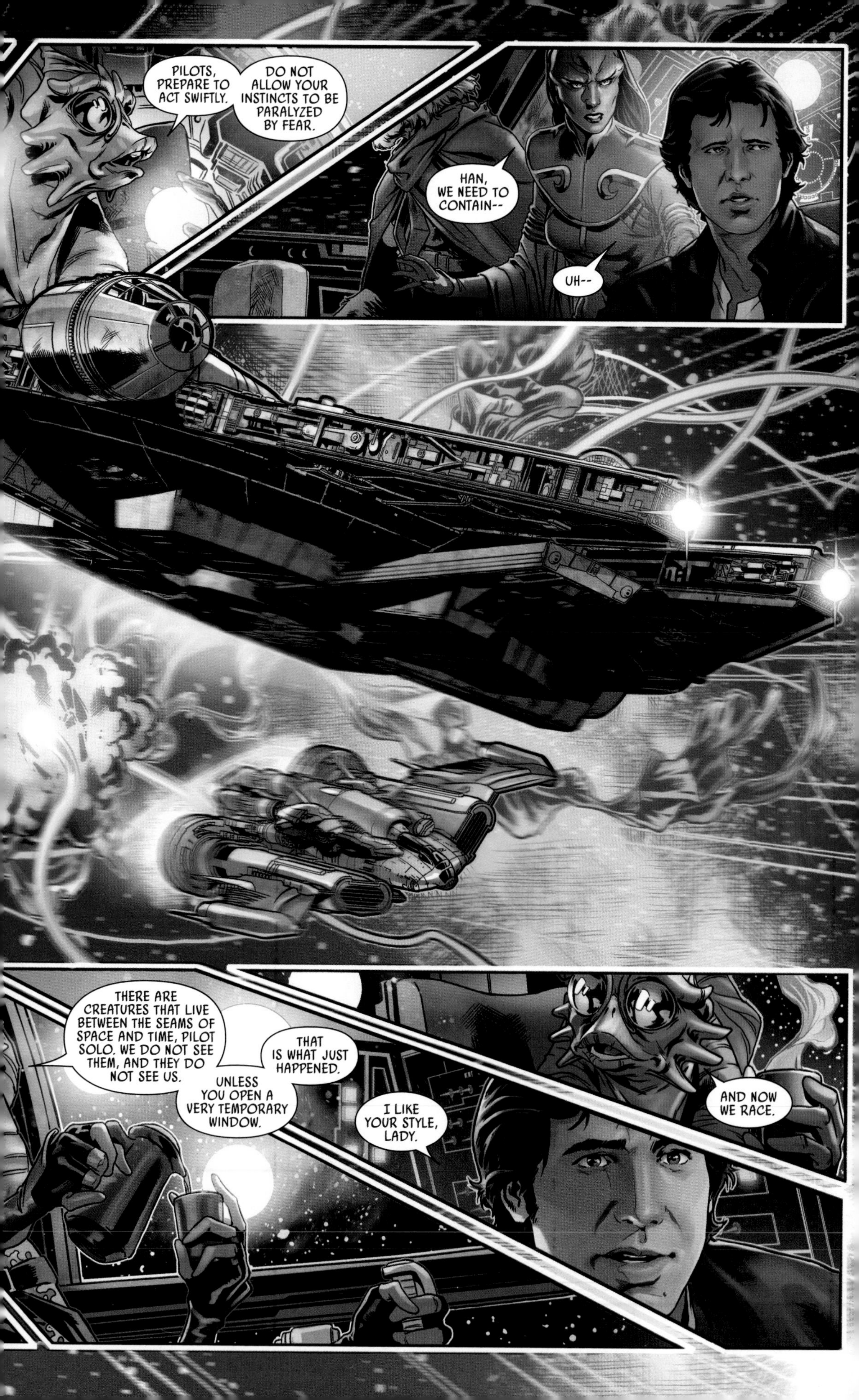
PILOTS, PREPARE TO ACT SWIFTLY.
DO NOT ALLOW YOUR INSTINCTS TO BE PARALYZED BY FEAR.
HAN, WE NEED TO CONTAIN--
UH--
THERE ARE CREATURES THAT LIVE BETWEEN THE SEAMS OF SPACE AND TIME, PILOT SOLO. WE DO NOT SEE THEM, AND THEY DO NOT SEE US.
UNLESS YOU OPEN A VERY TEMPORARY WINDOW.
THAT IS WHAT JUST HAPPENED.
I LIKE YOUR STYLE, LADY.
AND NOW WE RACE.

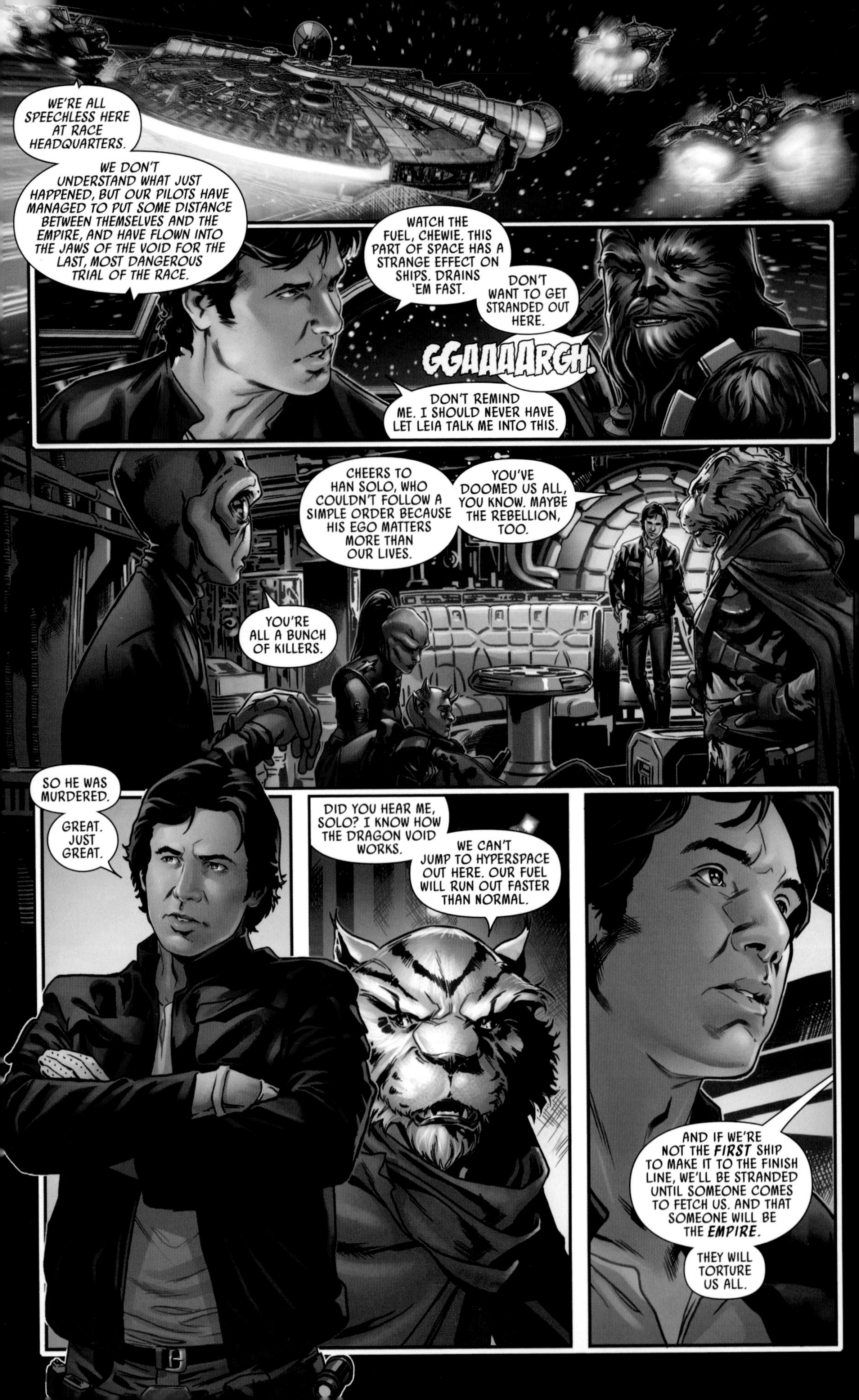
WE'RE ALL SPEECHLESS HERE AT RACE HEADQUARTERS.
WE DON'T UNDERSTAND WHAT JUST HAPPENED, BUT OUR PILOTS HAVE MANAGED TO PUT SOME DISTANCE BETWEEN THEMSELVES AND THE EMPIRE, AND HAVE FLOWN INTO THE JAWS OF THE VOID FOR THE LAST, MOST DANGEROUS TRIAL OF THE RACE.
WATCH THE FUEL, CHEWIE. THIS PART OF SPACE HAS A STRANGE EFFECT ON SHIPS. DRAINS 'EM FAST.
DON'T WANT TO GET STRANDED OUT HERE.
GGAAAARGH!
DON'T REMIND ME. I SHOULD NEVER HAVE LET LEIA TALK ME INTO THIS.
CHEERS TO HAN SOLO, WHO COULDN'T FOLLOW A SIMPLE ORDER BECAUSE HIS EGO MATTERS MORE THAN OUR LIVES.
YOU'VE DOOMED US ALL, YOU KNOW. MAYBE THE REBELLION, TOO.
YOU'RE ALL A BUNCH OF KILLERS.
SO HE WAS MURDERED.
GREAT. JUST GREAT.
DID YOU HEAR ME, SOLO? I KNOW HOW THE DRAGON VOID WORKS.
WE CAN'T JUMP TO HYPERSPACE OUT HERE. OUR FUEL WILL RUN OUT FASTER THAN NORMAL.
AND IF WE'RE NOT THE FIRST SHIP TO MAKE IT TO THE FINISH LINE, WE'LL BE STRANDED UNTIL SOMEONE COMES TO FETCH US. AND THAT SOMEONE WILL BE THE EMPIRE.
THEY WILL TORTURE US ALL.

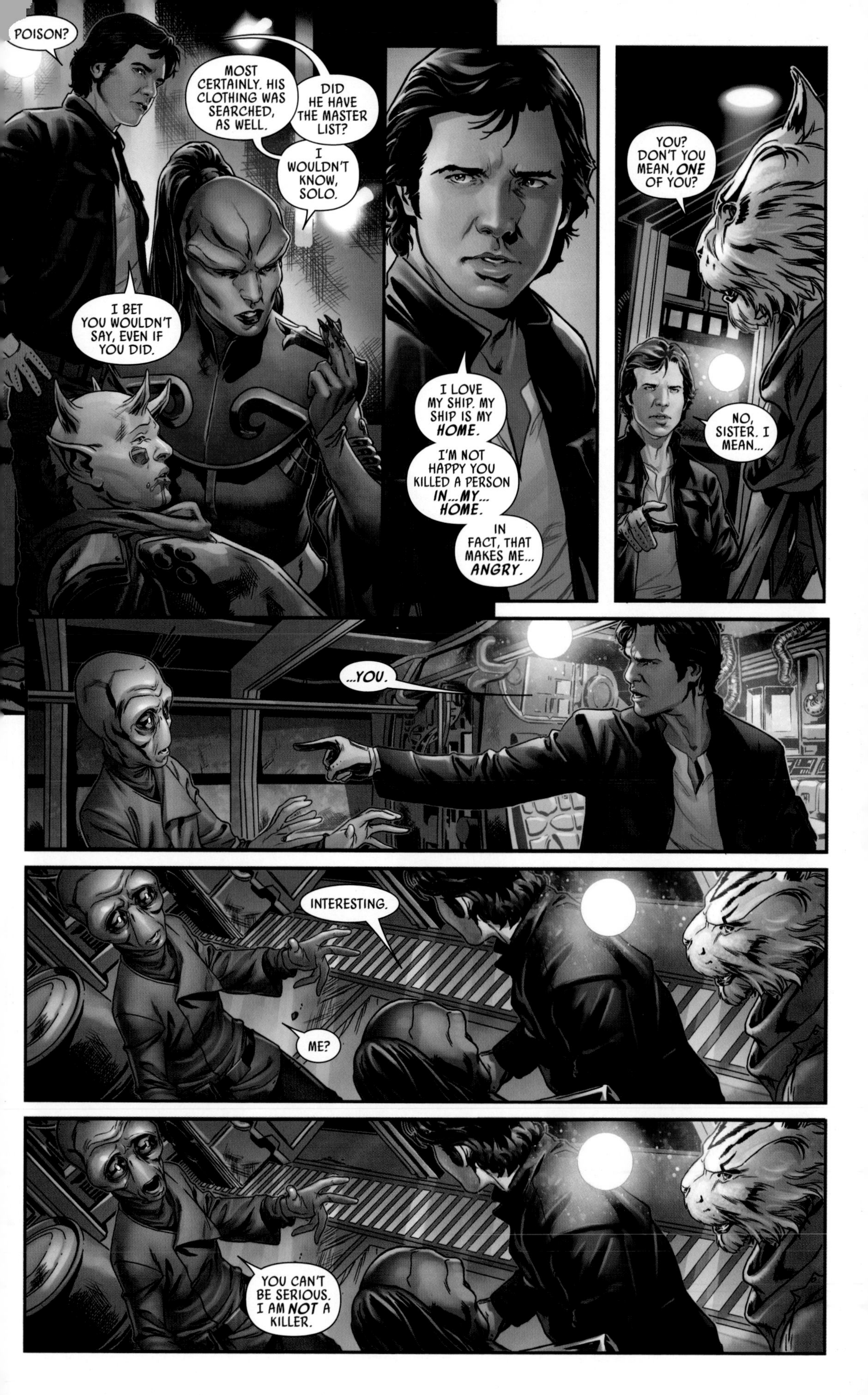
POISON?
MOST CERTAINLY. HIS CLOTHING WAS SEARCHED, AS WELL.
DID HE HAVE THE MASTER LIST?
I WOULDN'T KNOW, SOLO.
I BET YOU WOULDN'T SAY, EVEN IF YOU DID.
I LOVE MY SHIP. MY SHIP IS MY HOME.
I'M NOT HAPPY YOU KILLED A PERSON IN...MY... HOME.
IN FACT, THAT MAKES ME... ANGRY.
YOU? DON'T YOU MEAN, ONE OF YOU?
NO, SISTER. I MEAN...
...YOU.
INTERESTING.
ME?
YOU CAN'T BE SERIOUS. I AM NOT A KILLER.

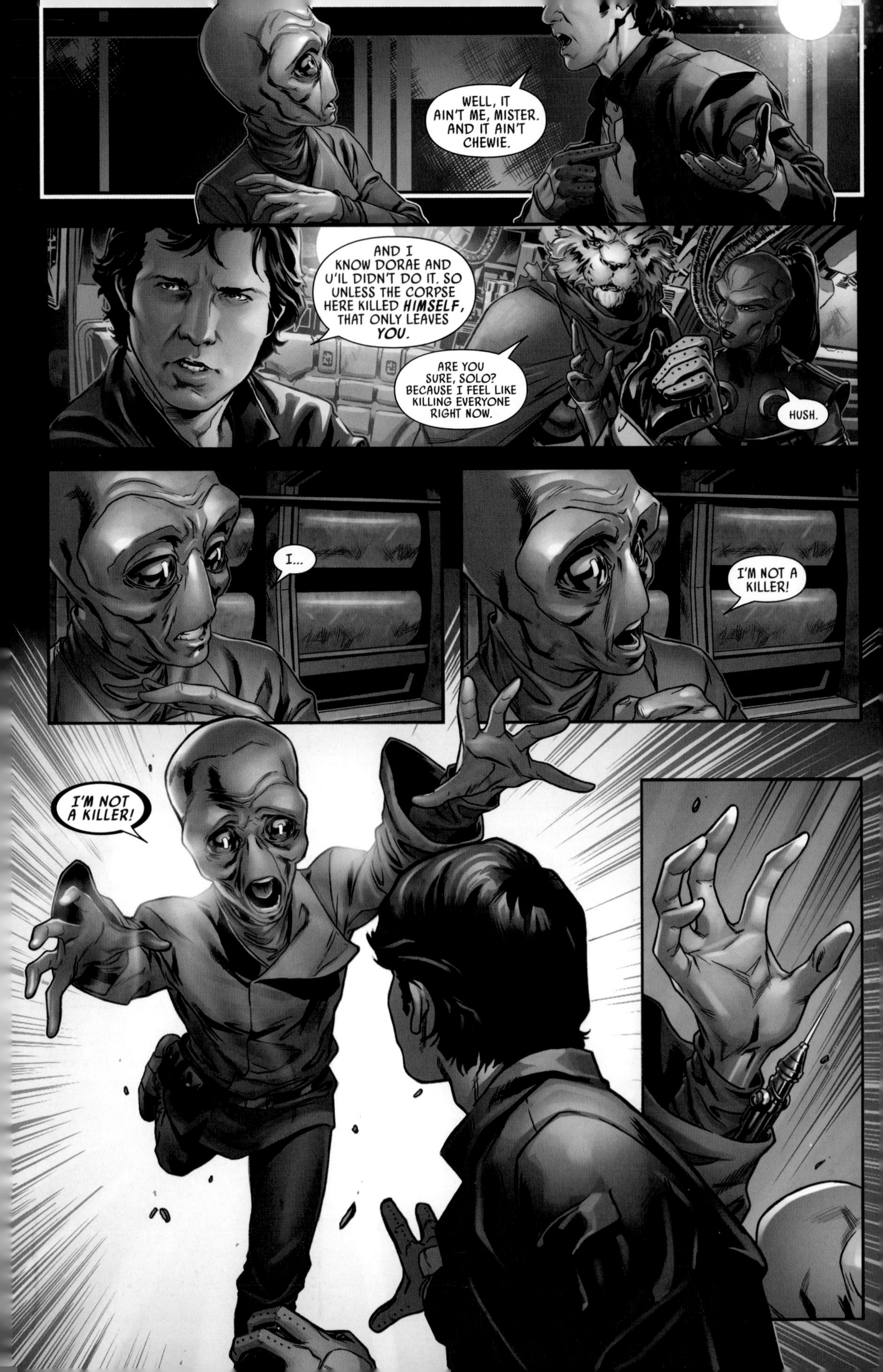
WELL, IT AIN'T ME, MISTER. AND IT AIN'T CHEWIE.
AND I KNOW DORAE AND U'IL DIDN'T DO IT. SO UNLESS THE CORPSE HERE KILLED **HIMSELF**, THAT ONLY LEAVES **YOU**.
ARE YOU SURE, SOLO? BECAUSE I FEEL LIKE KILLING EVERYONE RIGHT NOW.
HUSH.
I...
I'M NOT A KILLER!
I'M NOT A KILLER!

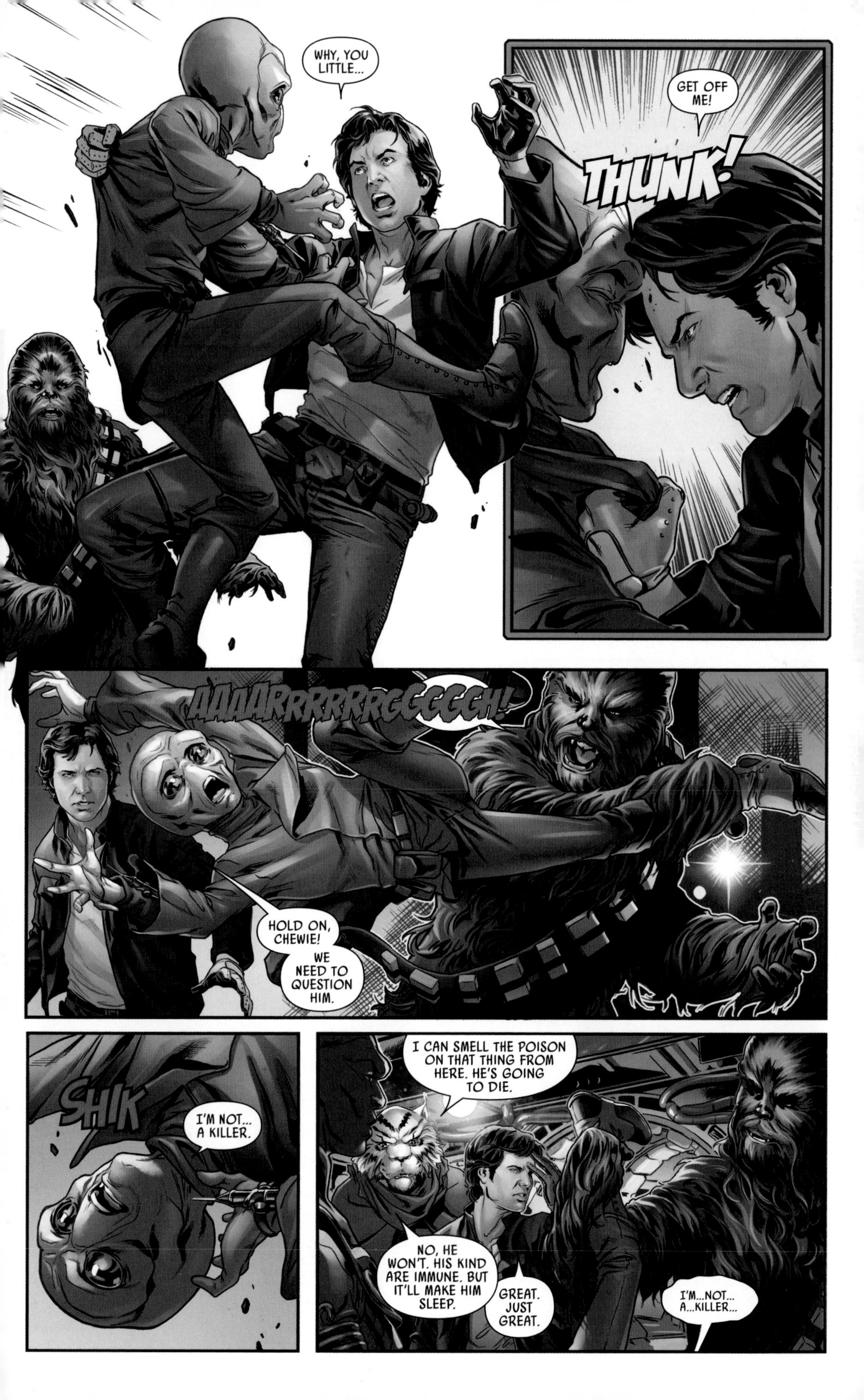

WHY, YOU LITTLE...
GET OFF ME!
THUNK!
AAAARRRRRRGGGGGH!
HOLD ON, CHEWIE!
WE NEED TO QUESTION HIM.
SHIK
I'M NOT... A KILLER.
I CAN SMELL THE POISON ON THAT THING FROM HERE. HE'S GOING TO DIE.
NO, HE WON'T. HIS KIND ARE IMMUNE. BUT IT'LL MAKE HIM SLEEP.
GREAT. JUST GREAT.
I'M...NOT... A...KILLER...

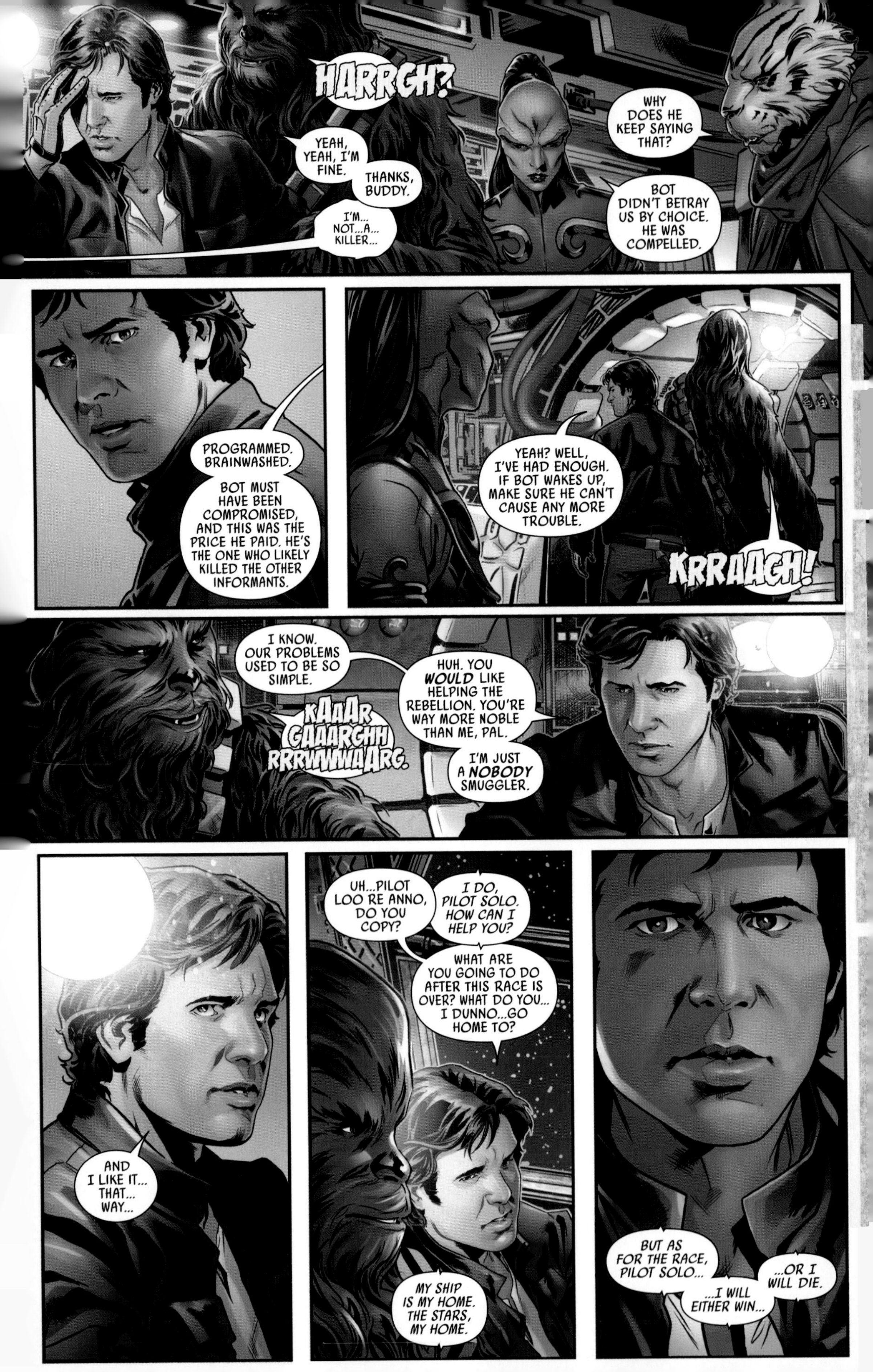
HARRGH?
YEAH, YEAH, I'M FINE.
THANKS, BUDDY.
I'M... NOT...A... KILLER...
WHY DOES HE KEEP SAYING THAT?
BOT DIDN'T BETRAY US BY CHOICE. HE WAS COMPELLED.
PROGRAMMED. BRAINWASHED.
BOT MUST HAVE BEEN COMPROMISED, AND THIS WAS THE PRICE HE PAID. HE'S THE ONE WHO LIKELY KILLED THE OTHER INFORMANTS.
YEAH? WELL, I'VE HAD ENOUGH. IF BOT WAKES UP, MAKE SURE HE CAN'T CAUSE ANY MORE TROUBLE.
KRRAAGH!
KAAAR GAAARGHH RRRWWWAARG.
I KNOW. OUR PROBLEMS USED TO BE SO SIMPLE.
HUH. YOU WOULD LIKE HELPING THE REBELLION. YOU'RE WAY MORE NOBLE THAN ME, PAL.
I'M JUST A NOBODY SMUGGLER.
AND I LIKE IT... THAT... WAY...
UH...PILOT LOO RE ANNO, DO YOU COPY?
I DO, PILOT SOLO. HOW CAN I HELP YOU?
WHAT ARE YOU GOING TO DO AFTER THIS RACE IS OVER? WHAT DO YOU... I DUNNO...GO HOME TO?
MY SHIP IS MY HOME. THE STARS, MY HOME.
BUT AS FOR THE RACE, PILOT SOLO...
...I WILL EITHER WIN...
...OR I WILL DIE.

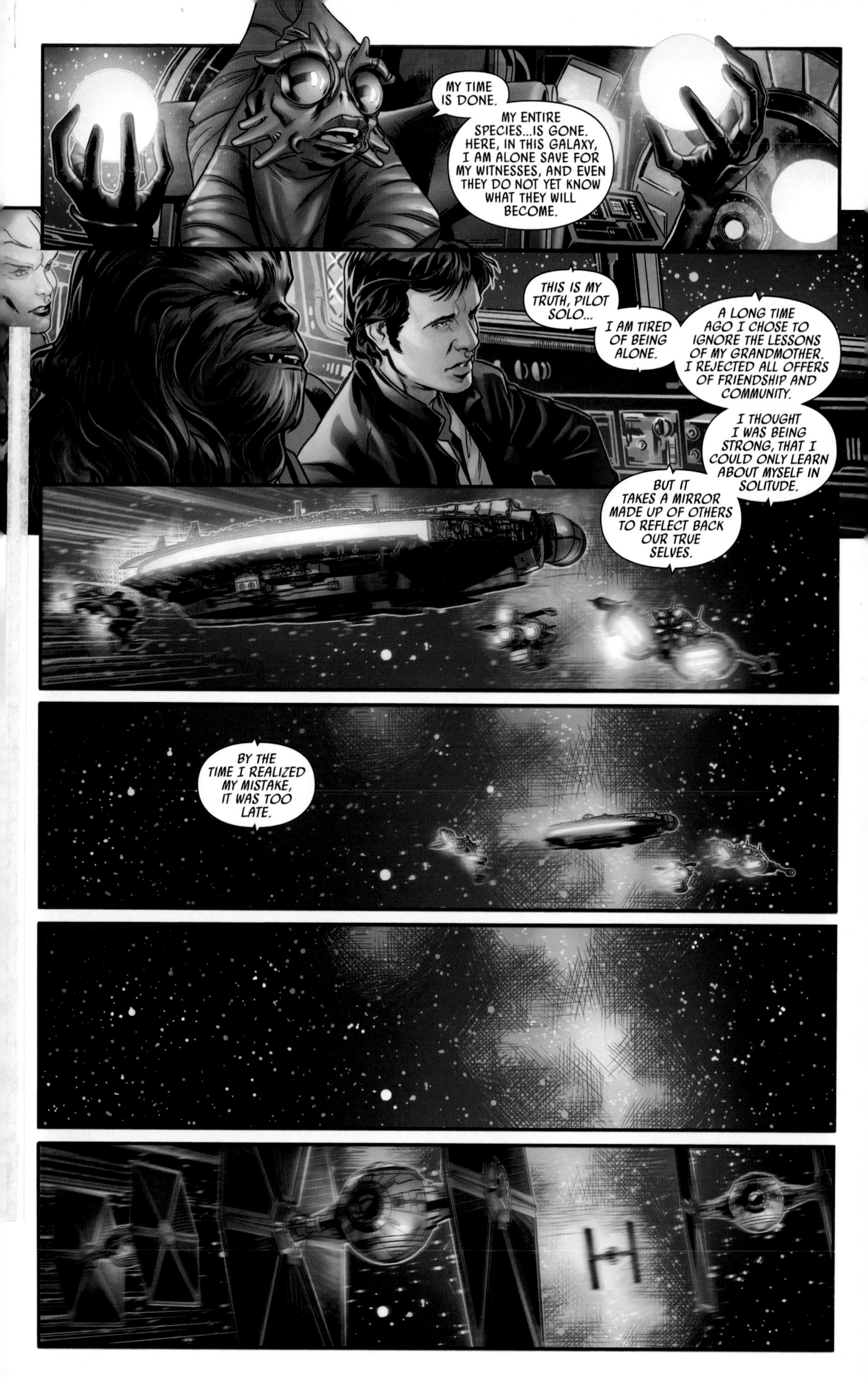

MY TIME IS DONE.
MY ENTIRE SPECIES...IS GONE. HERE, IN THIS GALAXY, I AM ALONE SAVE FOR MY WITNESSES, AND EVEN THEY DO NOT YET KNOW WHAT THEY WILL BECOME.
THIS IS MY TRUTH, PILOT SOLO...
I AM TIRED OF BEING ALONE.
A LONG TIME AGO I CHOSE TO IGNORE THE LESSONS OF MY GRANDMOTHER. I REJECTED ALL OFFERS OF FRIENDSHIP AND COMMUNITY.
I THOUGHT I WAS BEING STRONG, THAT I COULD ONLY LEARN ABOUT MYSELF IN SOLITUDE.
BUT IT TAKES A MIRROR MADE UP OF OTHERS TO REFLECT BACK OUR TRUE SELVES.
BY THE TIME I REALIZED MY MISTAKE, IT WAS TOO LATE.

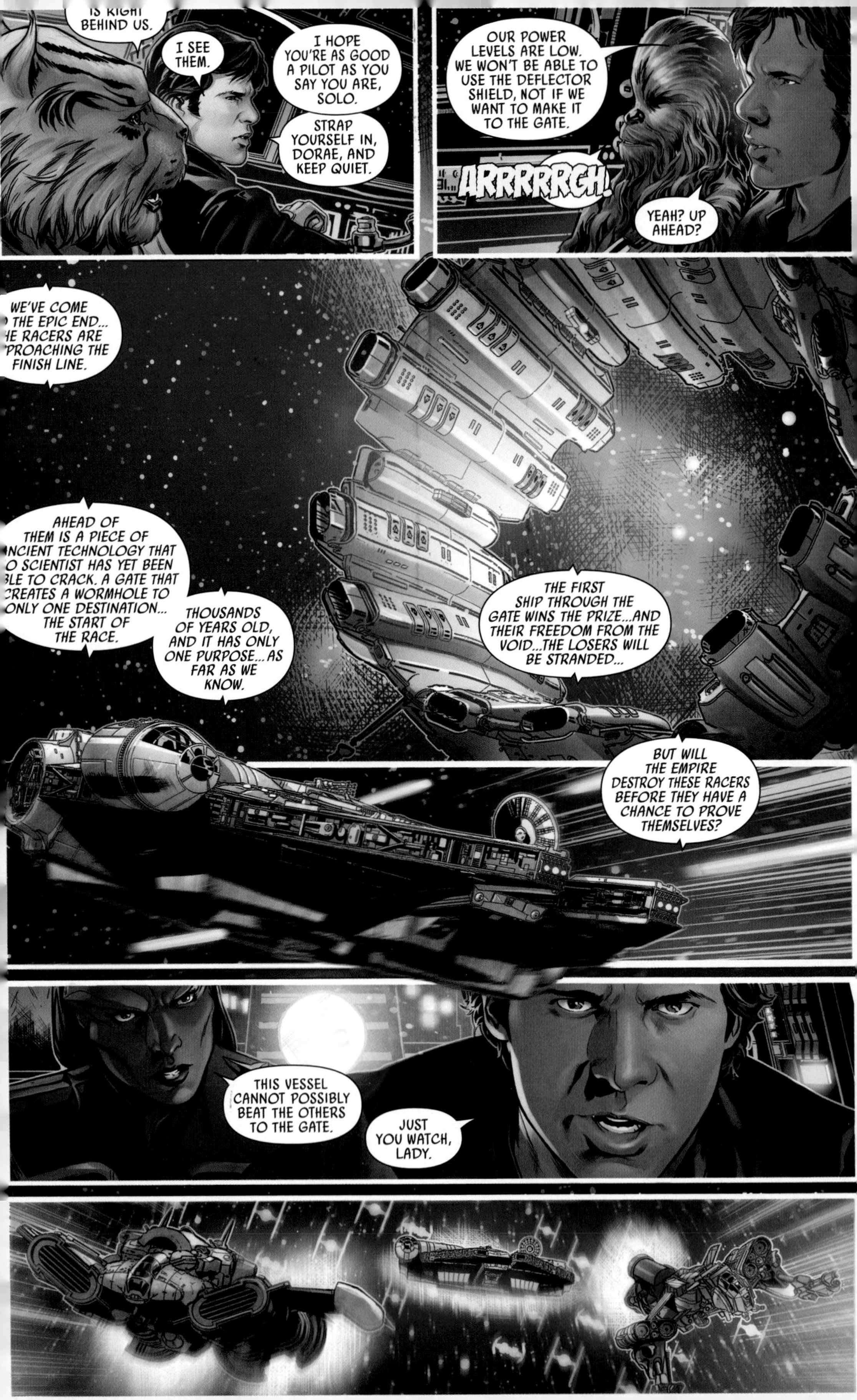
IS RIGHT BEHIND US.
I SEE THEM.
I HOPE YOU'RE AS GOOD A PILOT AS YOU SAY YOU ARE, SOLO.
STRAP YOURSELF IN, DORAE, AND KEEP QUIET.
OUR POWER LEVELS ARE LOW. WE WON'T BE ABLE TO USE THE DEFLECTOR SHIELD, NOT IF WE WANT TO MAKE IT TO THE GATE.
ARRRRRGH!
YEAH? UP AHEAD?
WE'VE COME THE EPIC END... HE RACERS ARE PROACHING THE FINISH LINE.
AHEAD OF THEM IS A PIECE OF NCIENT TECHNOLOGY THAT O SCIENTIST HAS YET BEEN BLE TO CRACK. A GATE THAT CREATES A WORMHOLE TO ONLY ONE DESTINATION... THE START OF THE RACE.
THOUSANDS OF YEARS OLD, AND IT HAS ONLY ONE PURPOSE... AS FAR AS WE KNOW.
THE FIRST SHIP THROUGH THE GATE WINS THE PRIZE...AND THEIR FREEDOM FROM THE VOID...THE LOSERS WILL BE STRANDED...
BUT WILL THE EMPIRE DESTROY THESE RACERS BEFORE THEY HAVE A CHANCE TO PROVE THEMSELVES?
THIS VESSEL CANNOT POSSIBLY BEAT THE OTHERS TO THE GATE.
JUST YOU WATCH, LADY.

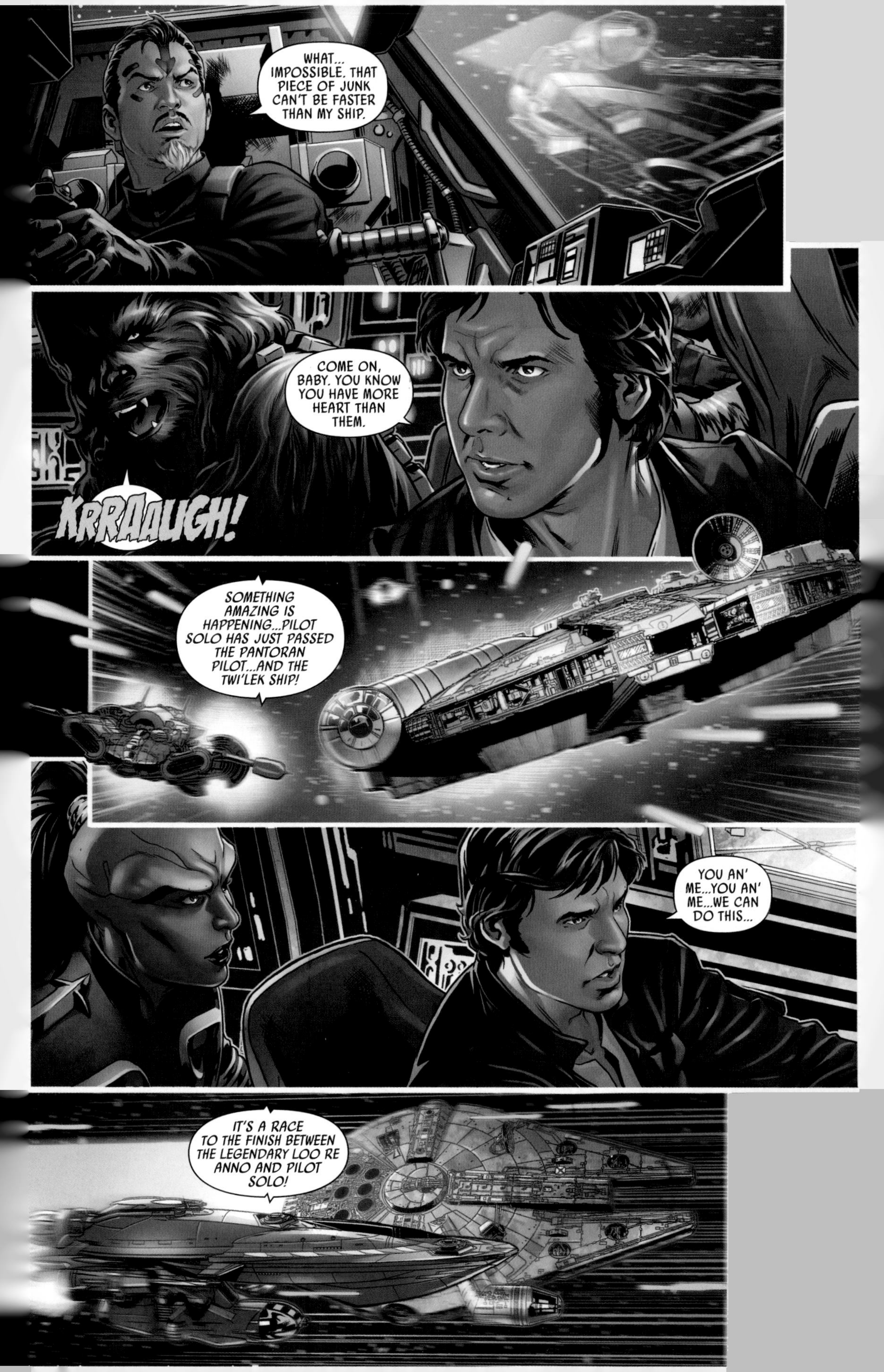
WHAT... IMPOSSIBLE. THAT PIECE OF JUNK CAN'T BE FASTER THAN MY SHIP.
COME ON, BABY. YOU KNOW YOU HAVE MORE HEART THAN THEM.
KRRAAUGH!
SOMETHING AMAZING IS HAPPENING...PILOT SOLO HAS JUST PASSED THE PANTORAN PILOT...AND THE TWI'LEK SHIP!
YOU AN' ME...YOU AN' ME...WE CAN DO THIS...
IT'S A RACE TO THE FINISH BETWEEN THE LEGENDARY LOO RE ANNO AND PILOT SOLO!

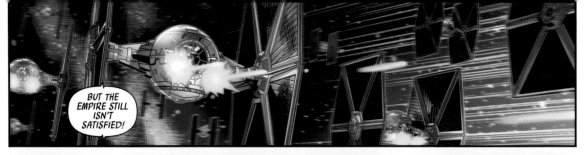

BUT THE EMPIRE STILL ISN'T SATISFIED!

THEY'RE SHOOTING TO KILL! RIGGING THIS RACE TO FAIL!

NO! LOO RE ANNO'S SHIP HAS BEEN HIT! I REPEAT, HER SHIP HAS BEEN HIT!

SHE'S FALLING BEHIND! PILOT SOLO IS GOING TO WIN THE DRAGON VOID!

YES...

I CAN'T BELIEVE IT...THIS OLD RUST BUCKET MADE IT...

BUT THAT MEANS...

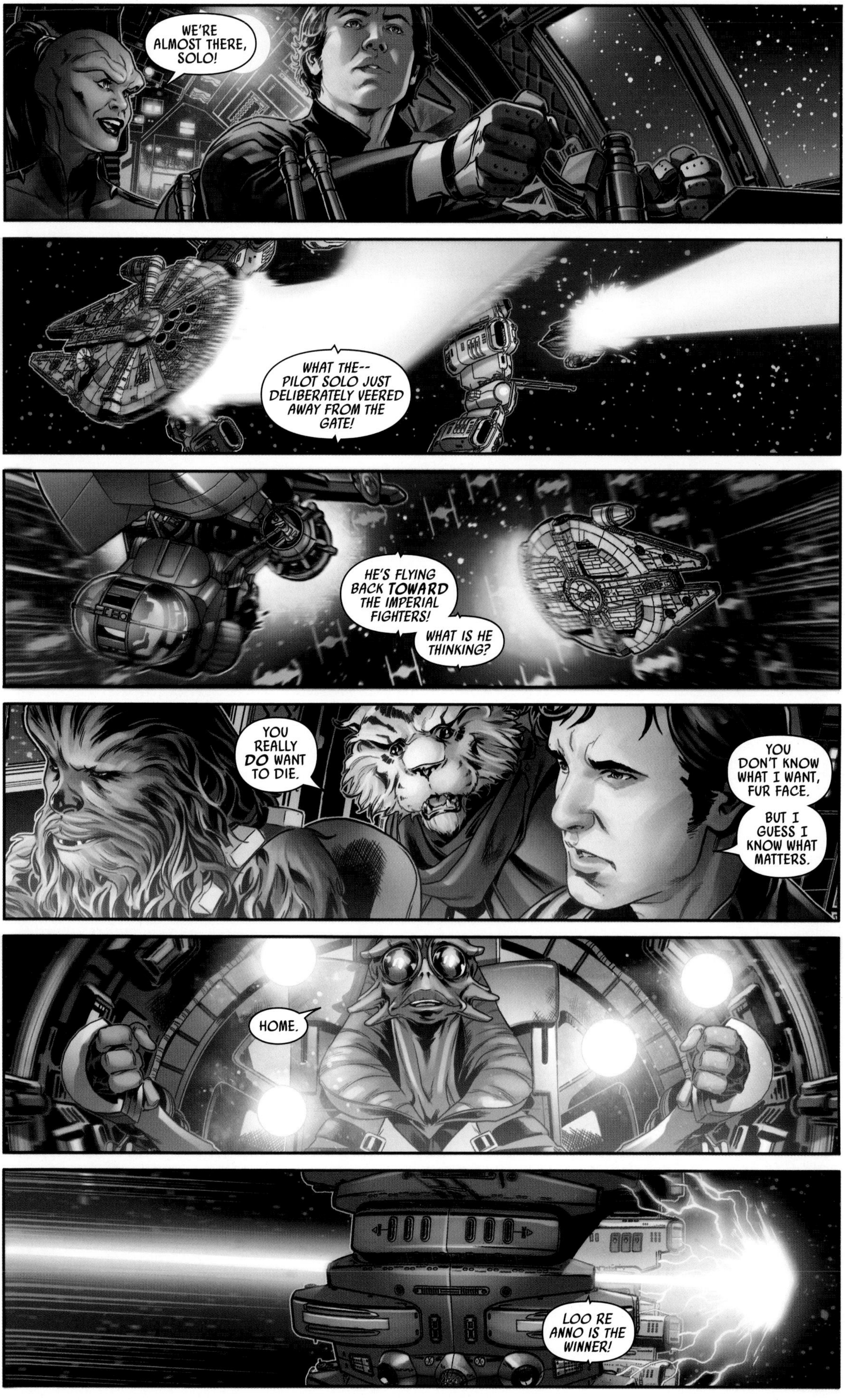
WE'RE ALMOST THERE, SOLO!
WHAT THE-- PILOT SOLO JUST DELIBERATELY VEERED AWAY FROM THE GATE!
HE'S FLYING BACK TOWARD THE IMPERIAL FIGHTERS!
WHAT IS HE THINKING?
YOU REALLY DO WANT TO DIE.
YOU DON'T KNOW WHAT I WANT, FUR FACE.
BUT I GUESS I KNOW WHAT MATTERS.
HOME.
LOO RE ANNO IS THE WINNER!

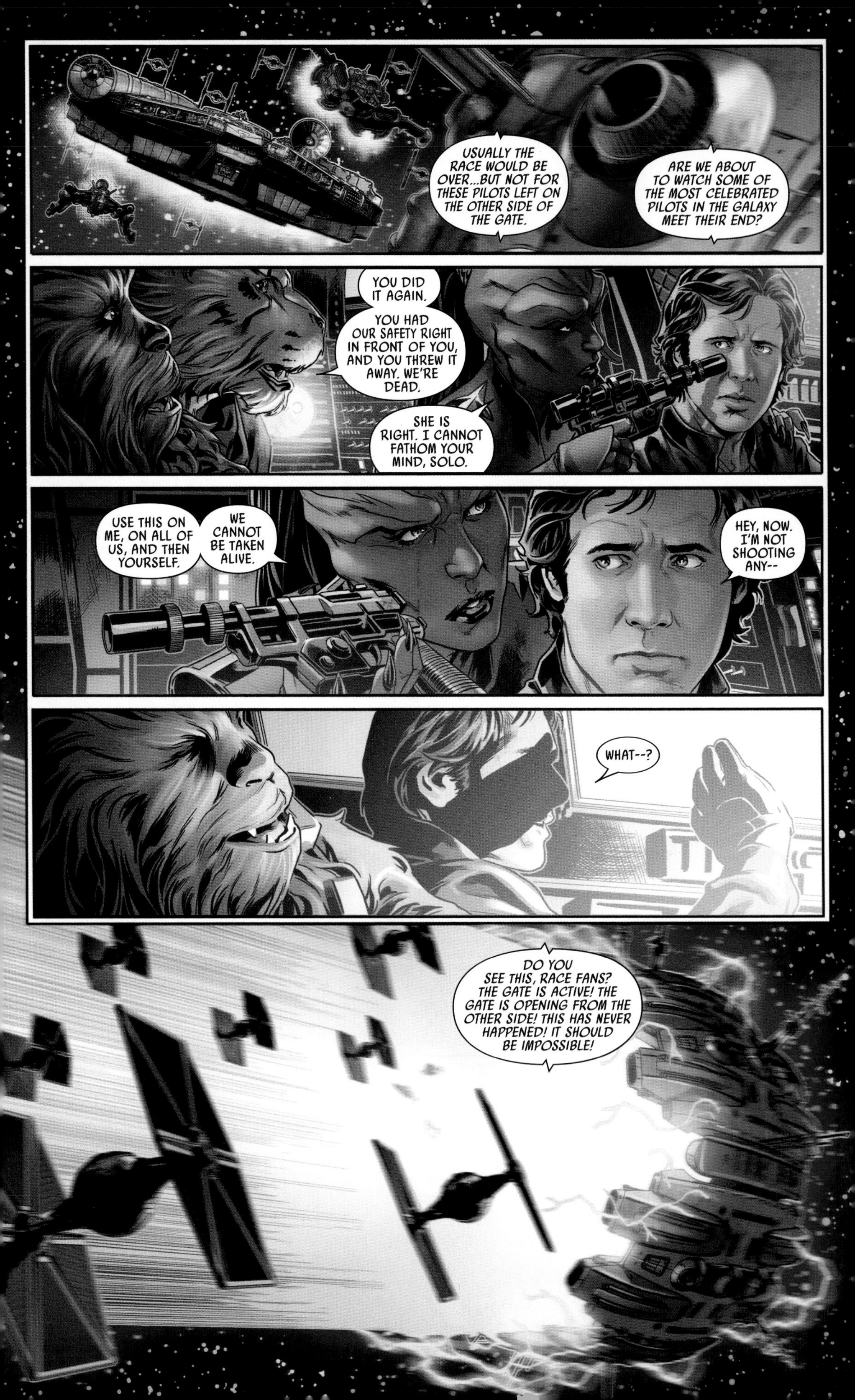
USUALLY THE RACE WOULD BE OVER...BUT NOT FOR THESE PILOTS LEFT ON THE OTHER SIDE OF THE GATE.
ARE WE ABOUT TO WATCH SOME OF THE MOST CELEBRATED PILOTS IN THE GALAXY MEET THEIR END?
YOU DID IT AGAIN.
YOU HAD OUR SAFETY RIGHT IN FRONT OF YOU, AND YOU THREW IT AWAY. WE'RE DEAD.
SHE IS RIGHT. I CANNOT FATHOM YOUR MIND, SOLO.
USE THIS ON ME, ON ALL OF US, AND THEN YOURSELF.
WE CANNOT BE TAKEN ALIVE.
HEY, NOW. I'M NOT SHOOTING ANY--
WHAT--?
DO YOU SEE THIS, RACE FANS? THE GATE IS ACTIVE! THE GATE IS OPENING FROM THE OTHER SIDE! THIS HAS NEVER HAPPENED! IT SHOULD BE IMPOSSIBLE!

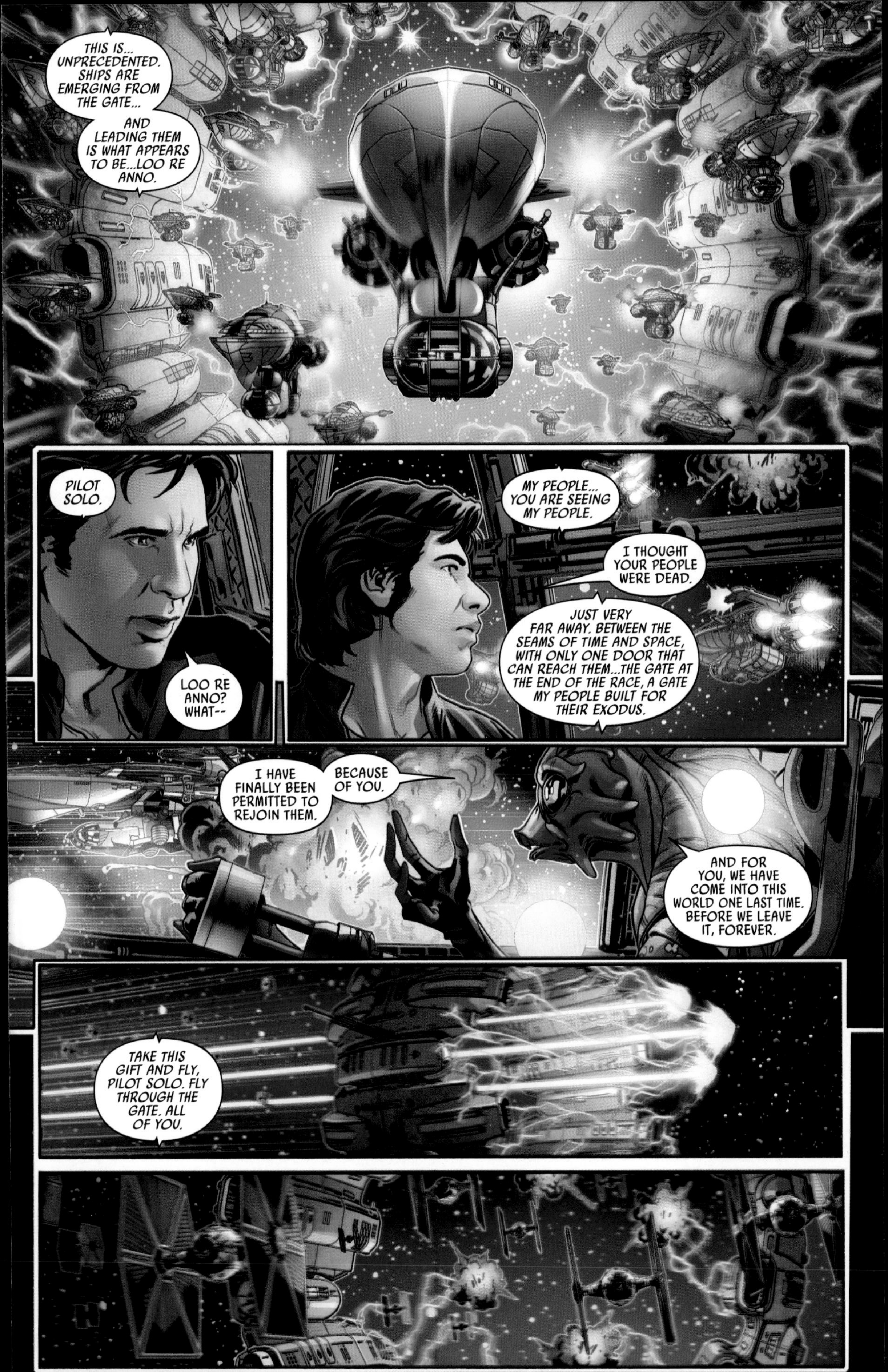
THIS IS... UNPRECEDENTED. SHIPS ARE EMERGING FROM THE GATE...
AND LEADING THEM IS WHAT APPEARS TO BE...LOO RE ANNO.
PILOT SOLO.
LOO RE ANNO? WHAT--
MY PEOPLE... YOU ARE SEEING MY PEOPLE.
I THOUGHT YOUR PEOPLE WERE DEAD.
JUST VERY FAR AWAY. BETWEEN THE SEAMS OF TIME AND SPACE, WITH ONLY ONE DOOR THAT CAN REACH THEM...THE GATE AT THE END OF THE RACE, A GATE MY PEOPLE BUILT FOR THEIR EXODUS.
I HAVE FINALLY BEEN PERMITTED TO REJOIN THEM.
BECAUSE OF YOU.
AND FOR YOU, WE HAVE COME INTO THIS WORLD ONE LAST TIME. BEFORE WE LEAVE IT, FOREVER.
TAKE THIS GIFT AND FLY, PILOT SOLO. FLY THROUGH THE GATE. ALL OF YOU.

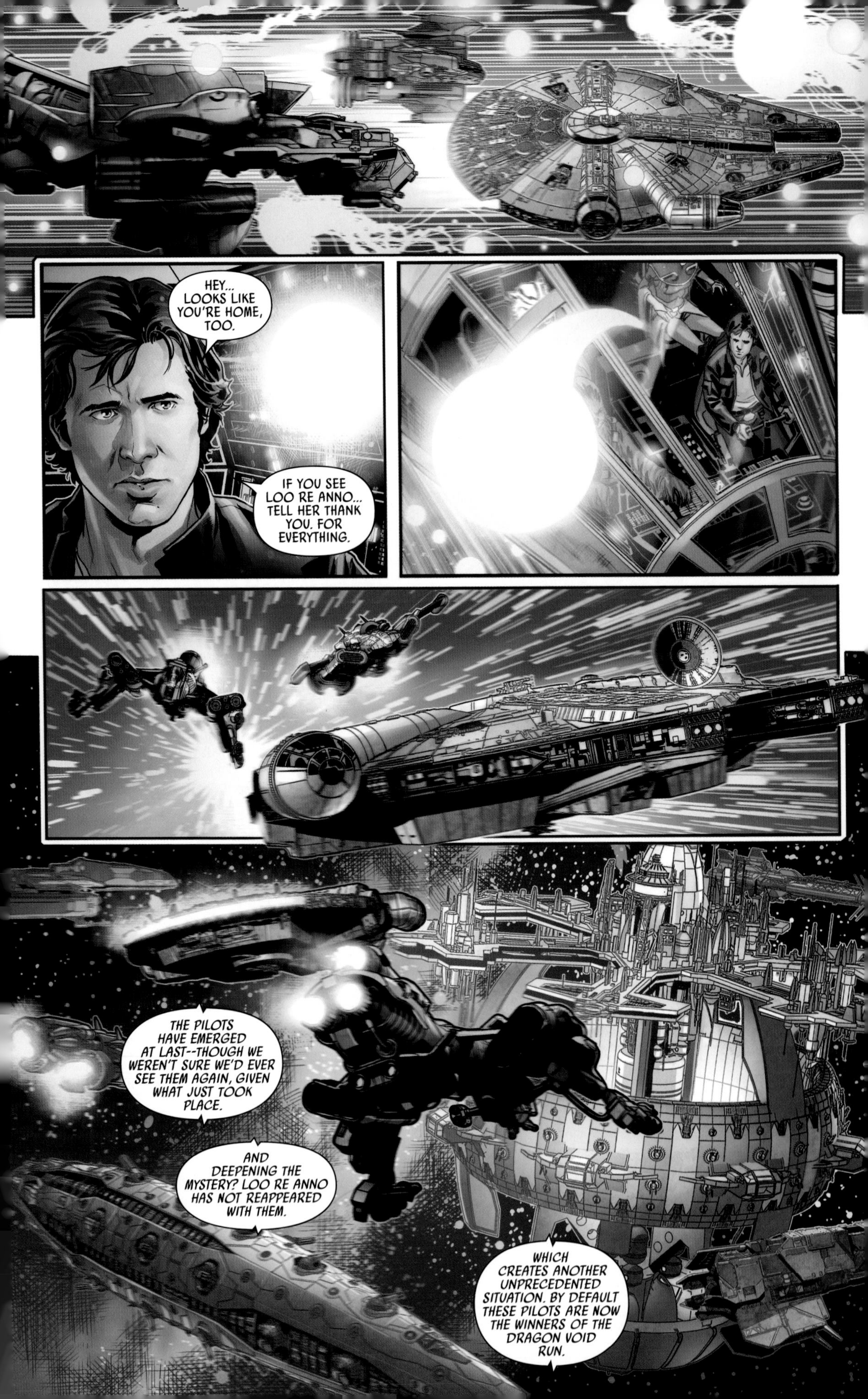
HEY... LOOKS LIKE YOU'RE HOME, TOO.
IF YOU SEE LOO RE ANNO... TELL HER THANK YOU. FOR EVERYTHING.
THE PILOTS HAVE EMERGED AT LAST--THOUGH WE WEREN'T SURE WE'D EVER SEE THEM AGAIN, GIVEN WHAT JUST TOOK PLACE.
AND DEEPENING THE MYSTERY? LOO RE ANNO HAS NOT REAPPEARED WITH THEM.
WHICH CREATES ANOTHER UNPRECEDENTED SITUATION. BY DEFAULT THESE PILOTS ARE NOW THE WINNERS OF THE DRAGON VOID RUN.

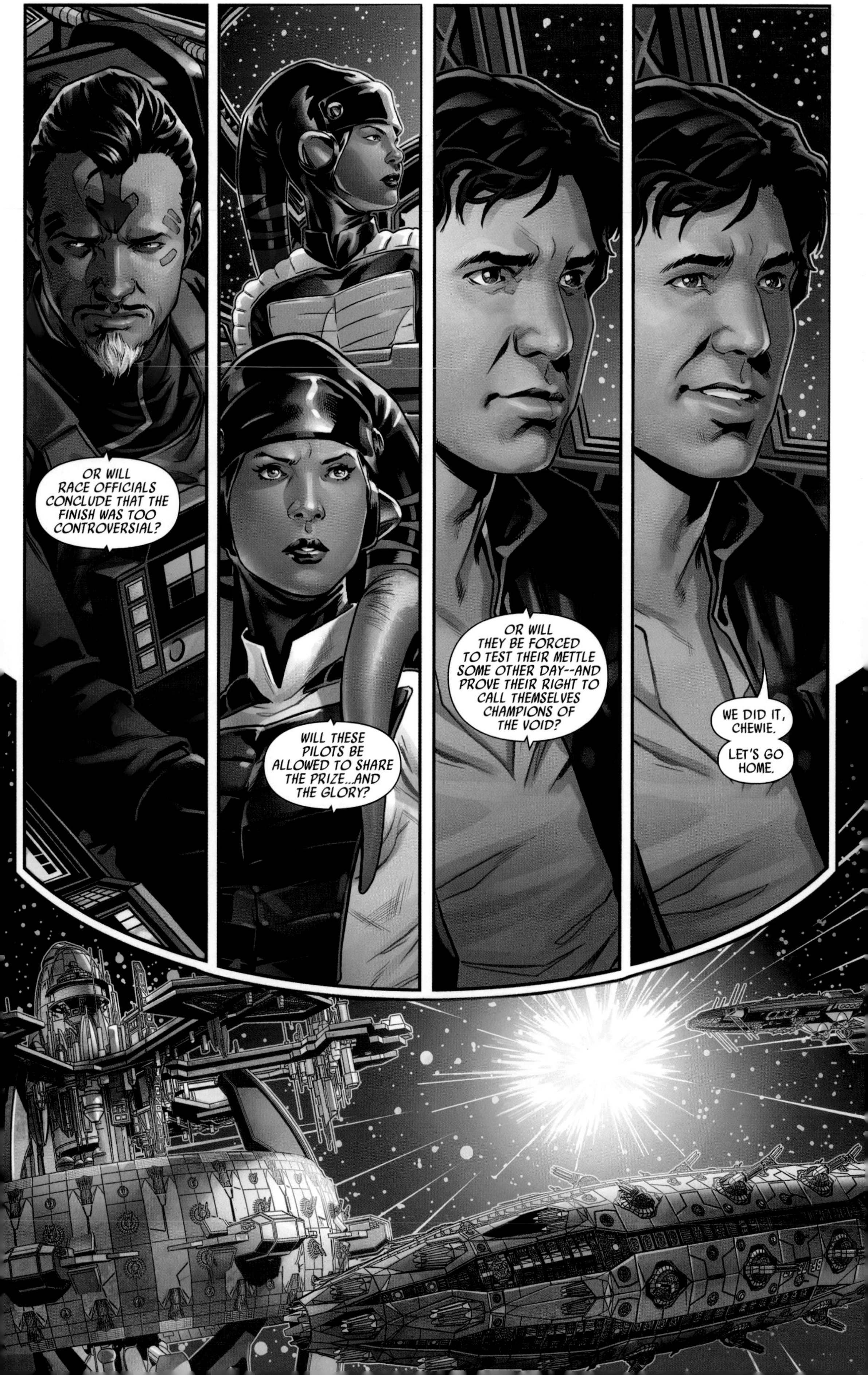
OR WILL RACE OFFICIALS CONCLUDE THAT THE FINISH WAS TOO CONTROVERSIAL?
WILL THESE PILOTS BE ALLOWED TO SHARE THE PRIZE...AND THE GLORY?
OR WILL THEY BE FORCED TO TEST THEIR METTLE SOME OTHER DAY--AND PROVE THEIR RIGHT TO CALL THEMSELVES CHAMPIONS OF THE VOID?
WE DID IT, CHEWIE.
LET'S GO HOME.

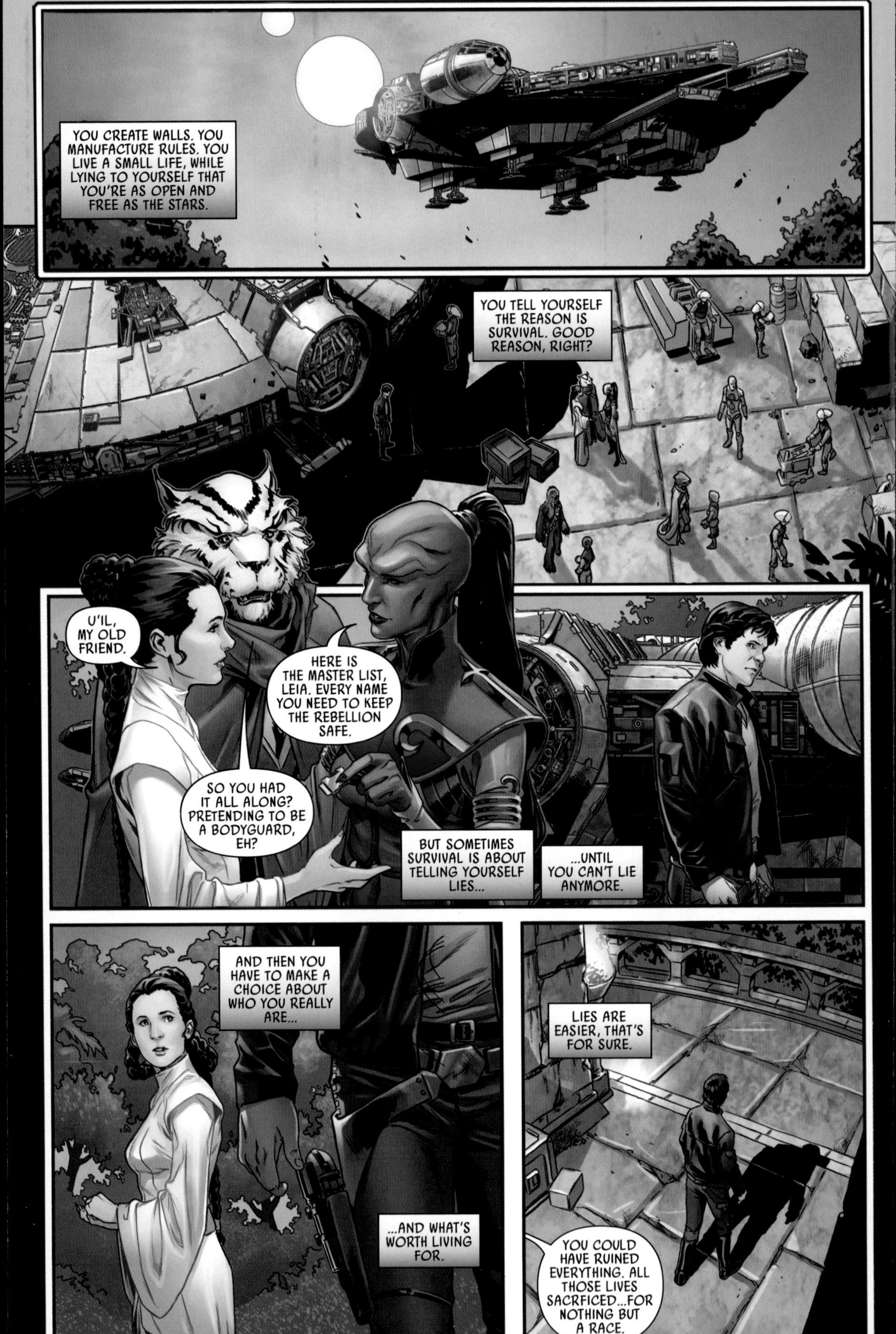
YOU CREATE WALLS. YOU MANUFACTURE RULES. YOU LIVE A SMALL LIFE, WHILE LYING TO YOURSELF THAT YOU'RE AS OPEN AND FREE AS THE STARS.
YOU TELL YOURSELF THE REASON IS SURVIVAL. GOOD REASON, RIGHT?
U'IL, MY OLD FRIEND.
HERE IS THE MASTER LIST, LEIA. EVERY NAME YOU NEED TO KEEP THE REBELLION SAFE.
SO YOU HAD IT ALL ALONG? PRETENDING TO BE A BODYGUARD, EH?
BUT SOMETIMES SURVIVAL IS ABOUT TELLING YOURSELF LIES...
...UNTIL YOU CAN'T LIE ANYMORE.
AND THEN YOU HAVE TO MAKE A CHOICE ABOUT WHO YOU REALLY ARE...
...AND WHAT'S WORTH LIVING FOR.
LIES ARE EASIER, THAT'S FOR SURE.
YOU COULD HAVE RUINED EVERYTHING. ALL THOSE LIVES SACRFICED...FOR NOTHING BUT A RACE.

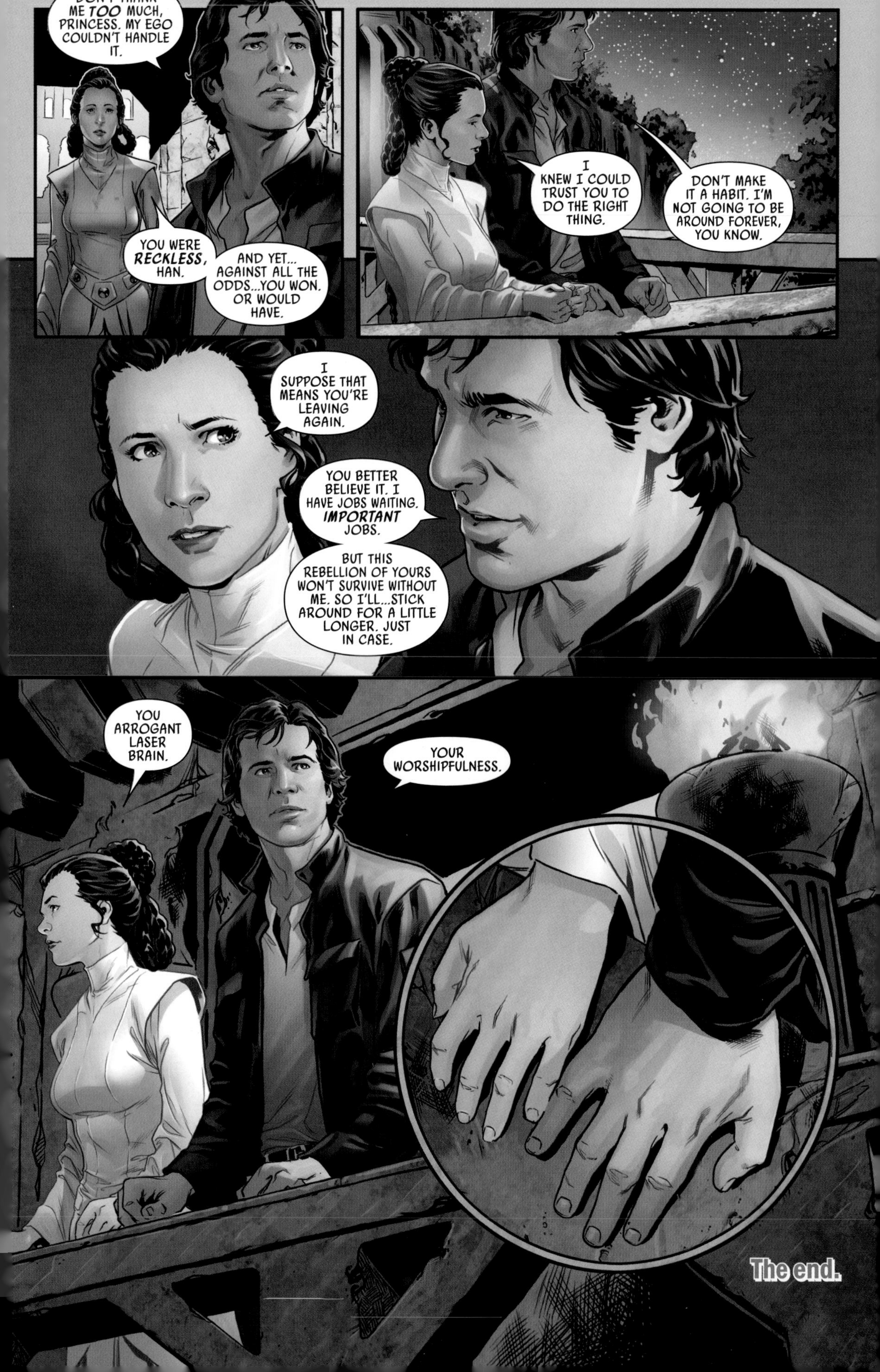
DON'T THANK ME TOO MUCH, PRINCESS. MY EGO COULDN'T HANDLE IT.
YOU WERE RECKLESS, HAN.
AND YET... AGAINST ALL THE ODDS...YOU WON. OR WOULD HAVE.
I KNEW I COULD TRUST YOU TO DO THE RIGHT THING.
DON'T MAKE IT A HABIT. I'M NOT GOING TO BE AROUND FOREVER, YOU KNOW.
I SUPPOSE THAT MEANS YOU'RE LEAVING AGAIN.
YOU BETTER BELIEVE IT. I HAVE JOBS WAITING. IMPORTANT JOBS.
BUT THIS REBELLION OF YOURS WON'T SURVIVE WITHOUT ME. SO I'LL...STICK AROUND FOR A LITTLE LONGER. JUST IN CASE.
YOU ARROGANT LASER BRAIN.
YOUR WORSHIPFULNESS.
The end.

# STAR WARS

# HAN SOLO

## COLLECT THEM ALL!
### Set of 5 Hardcover Books ISBN: 978-1-5321-4014-3

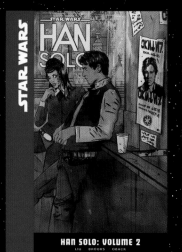

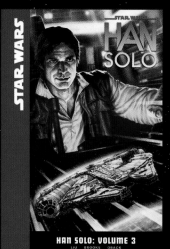

**Hardcover Book ISBN**
**978-1-5321-4015-0**

**Hardcover Book ISBN**
**978-1-5321-4016-7**

**Hardcover Book ISBN**
**978-1-5321-4017-4**

**Hardcover Book ISBN**
**978-1-5321-4018-1**

**Hardcover Book ISBN**
**978-1-5321-4019-8**